AMAZING WONDERS

STONEHENGE

BY MATT LILLEY

CREATIVE EDUCATION • CREATIVE PAPERBACKS

Published by Creative Education and Creative Paperbacks
P.O. Box 227, Mankato, Minnesota 56002
Creative Education and Creative Paperbacks
are imprints of The Creative Company
www.thecreativecompany.us

Design by The Design Lab
Art direction by Graham Morgan
Edited by Jill Kalz

Images by Getty (Karl Hendon, Valeriy Gavrilyuk), Pexels (John Nail, Kris Schulze, Kristian Thomas, Kyle Stehling, Lewis Ashton), Unsplash (Bryony Elena, Hulki Okan Tabak, Lenstravelier, Livin4wheel)

Library of Congress Cataloging-in-Publication Data
Names: Lilley, Matt, author.
Title: Stonehenge / Matt Lilley.
Description: Mankato, MN : Creative Education and Creative Paperbacks, [2025] | Series: Amazing wonders | Includes bibliographical references and index. | Audience: Ages 6–9 | Audience: Grades 2–3 | Summary: "An elementary-level introduction to Stonehenge, covering how, when, and why England's ancient wonder was created. Includes captions, on-page definitions, additional resources, and an index"—Provided by publisher.
Identifiers: LCCN 2023042437 (print) | LCCN 2023042438 (ebook) | ISBN 9781640268623 (library binding) | ISBN 9781682774120 (paperback) | ISBN 9798889890249 (ebook)
Subjects: LCSH: Stonehenge (England)—Juvenile literature.
Classification: LCC DA142 .L65 2025 (print) | LCC DA142 (ebook) | DDC 936.2/31—dc23/eng/20230909
LC record available at https://lccn.loc.gov/2023042437
LC ebook record available at https://lccn.loc.gov/2023042438

Printed in China

Table of Contents

The tallest stones stand 23 feet (7 meters).

The stones are laid out in circles. They're huge! The biggest stone weighs as much as two long school buses! Some stones are standing. Others have fallen. This **monument** is called Stonehenge.

monument a structure built to remember a person or event

The land on which Stonehenge sits is called Salisbury Plain.

Stonehenge is in southern England. It is on a flat, grassy plain. People can easily see it from far away. The stone circles are surrounded by a bank of earth and a ditch.

plain a large, flat area with no trees

Stonehenge is about the same age as the pyramids in Egypt. It was built in stages. The ditch was made around 2900 BC. Most of the stones were brought in about 400 years later.

Longer stones lying atop upright stones create doorways or windows.

Weather can wear away and weaken rock, causing it to fall.

The people who built Stonehenge left behind no writing.

Archeology is how we learn about them. We study the things they did leave behind. Old tools, bones, and other things can tell us how people lived.

archeology the study of history through the things people left behind

Stonehenge may have been built to honor the dead. Or it may be a giant calendar. On certain days, some stones line up with the sun. Others line up with the moon. People long ago used the sun and moon to track the seasons.

Stonehenge may have been a place to worship a sun god.

The stones at Stonehenge are not from nearby. They came from as far away as 180 miles (290 kilometers). People likely dragged the stones on wooden sleds or rails. To cross rivers, they may have put the stones on rafts.

Major repairs were made to the stones in the 1950s and 1960s.

To raise the stones, people first dug holes. They used picks made from deer antlers. Then they slid the stones into the holes and pulled them upright. The bottoms of the stones stayed buried.

Green plantlike organisms called lichens grow on the stones.

No one knows for sure how the lintels were placed on top. People may have used layers of wood to lift them little by little. The lintels have holes in them. These holes fit snugly on bumps atop the large stones.

lintels the long stones on top of the large stones

Stonehenge is a place of wonder. It is a window into the deep past. It gives us clues about the lives of people from long ago. We are still learning about them and the amazing things they did.

The summer solstice is the longest day of the year and a popular time to visit Stonehenge.

Wonder Spotlight: Bluestones

Bluestones

are smaller stones at Stonehenge that look blue when wet. In 2011, scientists discovered where they had come from. Chippings matched the stones in a Welsh mountain nearly 200 miles (322 km) away! Scientists found the exact spot where one bluestone came from. That stone was first moved around 3300 BC. It wasn't placed at Stonehenge, though, until 400 years later. It was probably used somewhere else first.

Read More

Davies, Monika. *England*. Minneapolis: Bellwether Media, 2023.

Gaertner, Meg. *Stonehenge*. Mendota Heights, Minn.: Apex, 2022.

Peterson, Megan Cooley. *Stonehenge: Who Built This Stone Formation?* Mankato, Minn.: Black Rabbit Books, 2019.

Websites

KidzSearch Encyclopedia: Stonehenge
https://wiki.kidzsearch.com/wiki/Stonehenge
Learn about the stones of Stonehenge.

National Geographic Kids: Stonehenge Facts!
https://www.natgeokids.com/uk/discover/history/general-history/stonehenge-facts/
Discover more facts about this wonder.

Note: Every effort has been made to ensure that the websites listed above are suitable for children, that they have educational value, and that they contain no inappropriate material. However, because of the nature of the Internet, it is impossible to guarantee that these sites will remain active indefinitely or that their contents will not be altered.

Index